DOVER
★ ★
CHILDREN'S THRIFT CLASSICS

The Story of the Nutcracker

E. T. A. HOFFMANN

Adapted by Bob Blaisdell
Illustrated by Thea Kliros

DOVER PUBLICATIONS, INC.
Mineola, New York

DOVER CHILDREN'S THRIFT CLASSICS
EDITOR OF THIS VOLUME: CANDACE WARD

Published in Canada by General Publishing Company, Ltd., 30 Lesmill Road, Don Mills, Toronto, Ontario.
Published in the United Kingdom by Constable and Company, Ltd., 3 The Lanchesters, 162–164 Fulham Palace Road, London W6 9ER.

Bibliographical Note

This Dover edition, first published in 1996, is a new abridgment, by Bob Blaisdell, based on "Nutcracker and the King of Mice" by E.T.A. Hoffmann, translated by Major Alexander Ewing, as published in *The Best Tales of Hoffmann* (New York: Dover Publications, Inc., 1967). The illustrations and introductory Note have been prepared specially for this edition.

Library of Congress Cataloging-in-Publication Data

Hoffmann, E. T. A. (Ernst Theodor Amadeus), 1776–1822.
    The story of the nutcracker / E. T. A. Hoffmann ; adapted by Bob Blaisdell ; illustrated by Thea Kliros.
       p.   cm. — (Dover children's thrift classics)
    A new ed. based on The nutcracker and the Mouse-King.
    Summary: After hearing how her toy nutcracker got his ugly face, a little girl helps break the spell and changes him into a handsome prince.
    ISBN 0-486-29153-7 (pbk.)
    [1. Fairy tales.] I. Blaisdell, Robert. II. Kliros, Thea, ill.
III. Hoffmann, E. T. A. (Ernst Theodor Amadeus), 1776–1822.
Nussknacker und Mausekönig. IV. Title. V. Series.
PZ8.H675Nt 1996
[Fic]—dc20   96–16373
                                                    CIP
                                                       AC

Manufactured in the United States of America
Dover Publications, Inc., 31 East 2nd Street, Mineola, N.Y. 11501

Note

ERNST THEODOR AMADEUS HOFFMANN (1776–1822) was one of the most prominent figures of nineteenth-century German literature and music. After studying law at the University of Königsberg, Hoffmann held a number of civil-service posts, but his true vocation was artistic. During his civil-service career, Hoffmann also made a name for himself in intellectual and artistic circles. His surviving musical works (many of his compositions have been lost) include ten operas, two symphonies, two masses, piano and chamber music, incidental music for plays and more.

Despite such a prolific musical output, Hoffmann is best known for his literary endeavors. His most famous works include stories such as "The Golden Flower Pot," "A New Year's Eve Adventure" and, of course, "Nutcracker and the King of Mice," upon which *The Story of the Nutcracker* is based. The original story, completed in 1816, first appeared in a collection of children's Christmas stories, *Kindermärchen von C. W. Contessa, Friedrich Baron de la Motte Fouqué und E. T. A. Hoffmann.* Though Hoffmann did not consider it a technical success—he felt it contained too many adult elements for a true children's story—it has become a perennial favorite with young and old alike.

Contents

The Story of
the Nutcracker

CHAPTER 1

Christmas Eve

O N THE TWENTY-FOURTH of December, Dr. Stahlbaum's children were not allowed at any time that day to go into the living-room. Fritz and Marie were sitting in a corner of the back parlor when the evening twilight fell. No candles were brought to that parlor, as was generally the case on Christmas Eve, and Fritz whispered to his young sister (who was just seven) that he had heard rattlings and rustlings going on all day, since early morning, inside the forbidden room, as well as distant hammering. He said he saw, a short time ago, a little dark-looking man slipping and creeping across the floor with a big box under his arm. At this news Marie clapped her little hands with joy, and cried:

"Oh! I do wonder what pretty things Godpapa Drosselmeier has been making for us *this* time!"

Godpapa Drosselmeier was anything but a nice-looking man. He was small and thin, with a great many wrinkles on his face, a big patch of black plaster where his right eye ought to have been, and not a hair on his head; this was why he wore a fine white wig made of glass. But he was a very, very clever man, who even understood all about clocks and watches, and could make them himself. So that when one of the beautiful clocks that were in Dr. Stahlbaum's house was out of sorts, Godpapa Drosselmeier would come, take off his wig and his little yellow coat, wrap an apron around himself, and stick sharp-pointed instruments into the clock. After this the poor clock would come to life again, and begin to whirr and sing and strike as merrily as ever. Of course, whenever he came he always brought something delightful in his pockets for the children—

perhaps a little man, who would comically roll his eyes and bow; or a box, out of which a little bird would jump; or something else of the kind. But for Christmas he always had some specially charming piece; something which had cost him much trouble— for which reason it was always taken away and put aside with the greatest care by the children's parents.

"Oh! what can Godpapa Drosselmeier have been making for us this time," Marie cried, as we have said.

Fritz thought that this time it could hardly be anything but a great castle, a fortress, where all sorts of handsome soldiers would be drilling and marching about; and then, that other soldiers would come and try to get into the fortress, upon which the soldiers inside would fire away at them with cannon, till everything banged and thundered like anything.

"No, no," Marie said. "Godpapa Drosselmeier once told me about a beautiful garden with a great lake in it, and beautiful swans swimming about with great gold collars, singing lovely music. And then a lovely little girl comes down through the garden to the lake, and calls the swans and feeds them with shortbread and cake."

"Swans don't eat cake and shortbread," Fritz cried, rather rudely, "and Godpapa Drosselmeier couldn't make a whole garden. After all, we have got very few of his playthings; whatever he brings is always taken away from us. So I like the things papa and mamma

give us much better; we keep them ourselves, and can do what we like with them."

The children went on discussing what he might have in store for them this time. Marie called Fritz's attention to the fact that Miss Gertrude (her biggest doll) was more clumsy and awkward than ever, tumbling on to the floor every so often. This did not occur without leaving marks on her face. Perhaps Marie would receive a new doll? Fritz, thinking of his own hopes, remarked that a good fox was needed for

his zoo collection, and that his army was quite without cavalry, as his papa was well aware. Marie sat in
thoughtful silence, but Fritz murmured quietly to
himself:

"Yes, I would like a fox and some cavalry men!"

It was now quite dark. Fritz and Marie, sitting close
together, did not dare to utter another sound; very
distant, but beautiful music could dimly be heard.
Then a bright gleam of light passed quickly across
the wall, and the children knew that the Christ Child
had sped away on shining wings to other happy
children. At this moment a silvery bell said, "Kling-
ling! Kling-ling!" the doors flew open, and such a
brilliant light came streaming from the living-room
that the children stood rooted where they were with
cries of "Oh! Oh!"

Papa and mamma came and took their hands,
saying, "Come now, darlings, and see what the
blessed Christ Child has brought for you."

CHAPTER 2

The Christmas Presents

I ASK YOU, kind reader (or listener)—Fritz, Theodore, Max, or whatever your name may be—to remember your last Christmas, how glorious it was with its various delightful Christmas presents; and then perhaps you will be able to imagine the way the two children stood speechless with their eyes fixed on all the beautiful things; how after a while, Marie, with a sigh, cried, "Oh, how lovely! how lovely!" and Fritz gave several jumps of delight.

The children had certainly been very, very good and well-behaved all that year; never before had so many beautiful and delightful things been provided for them. The great Christmas tree on the table bore many apples of silver and gold, and all its branches were heavy with sugar almonds, colored bon-bons, and all sorts of things to eat. Perhaps the prettiest thing about this wonder-tree, however, was the fact that among its spreading branches hundreds of little candles glittered like stars, inviting the children to pluck its flowers and fruit. Oh, how many beautiful things there were! Marie gazed there at the most delicious dolls, and all kinds of toys, and (what was the prettiest thing of all) a little silk dress with

colored ribbons that hung upon a branch; she cried out several times, "Oh! what a lovely, lovely, darling little dress!" Fritz, in the meantime, had had two or three trials of how his new fox (which he had found tied to the table) could gallop and now stated that he seemed a wildish sort of brute; but, no matter, he felt sure he would soon get him tamed; and then he set to work to gather and train his new squadron of cavalry men, well-equipped, in red and gold uniforms, with silver swords, and mounted on shining white horses.

When the children had sobered down a little, and were beginning upon the beautiful picture books (which were open, so that you could see all sorts of beautiful flowers and people of every shade, to say nothing of lovely children playing), there came another tinkling of a bell, to announce the display of Godpapa Drosselmeier's Christmas present, which was on another table, against the wall, concealed by a curtain. When this curtain was drawn, what did the children see?

On a green lawn, bright with flowers, stood a castle with a great many shining windows and golden towers. A chime of bells was going on inside it; doors and windows opened, and you saw very small but beautiful ladies and gentlemen with plumed hats, and long robes down to their heels walking up and down in the rooms of it. In the central hall there were hundreds of little candles burning in silver chandeliers; children in little short jackets were dancing to

the chimes of the bells. A gentleman in an emerald-green cloak came to a window, made signs, and then disappeared inside again; also, even Godpapa Drosselmeier himself (but scarcely taller than papa's thumb) came now and then, and stood at the castle door, then went in again.

Fritz had been looking on with the rest at the beautiful castle and the people walking about and dancing in it, with his arms leant on the table; then he said:

"Godpapa Drosselmeier, let *me* go into your castle for a little while."

Drosselmeier answered that this could not possibly be done. He was right; it was silly of Fritz to want to go into a castle which was not so tall as himself, golden towers and all. And Fritz saw that this was so.

After a short time, as the ladies and gentlemen kept on walking about just in the same fashion, the children dancing, and the emerald man looking out at the same window, and Godpapa Drosselmeier coming to the door, Fritz cried:

"Godpapa Drosselmeier, please come out at that other door!"

"That can't be done, dear Fritz," answered Drosselmeier.

"Well," said Fritz, "make that green man that looks out so often walk about with the others."

"And that can't be done, either," said his godpapa, once more.

"Make the children come down, then," said Fritz. "I want to see them nearer."

"Nonsense, nothing of that sort can be done," cried Drosselmeier. "The machinery must work as it's doing now; it can't be changed, you know."

"Oh," said Fritz, "it can't, eh? Very well, then, Godpapa Drosselmeier, if your little creatures in the castle there can only always do the same thing, they're not worth much, and I think precious little of them! No, give me my cavalry men! They've got to go backwards and forwards just as I want them to."

With this he went off to the other table, and set his squadron of silver horses trotting here and there, wheeling and charging and slashing right and left to his heart's content. Marie had slipped away softly, too, for she was tired of the walking and dancing of the puppets in the castle, though, kind and gentle as she was, she did not like to show it as her brother did. Drosselmeier, somewhat annoyed, said to the parents, "After all, a piece of mechanism like this is not a matter for children, who don't understand it; I shall put my castle back in its box again." But mother came to the rescue, and made him show her the clever machinery which moved the figures, Drosselmeier taking it all to pieces, putting it together again, and this made him feel cheerful once again. So that he gave the children all sorts of delightful brown men and women with golden faces, hands and legs, which were made of gingerbread, and with which they were very happy.

Chapter 3

Marie's Pet and Protégé

THERE WAS A reason why Marie found it hard to come away from the table where the Christmas presents were laid out; and this was, that she had just noticed something there which she had not observed at first. At some distance from the tree, there was a most interesting little man.

His body was rather too tall and stout for his legs, which were short and slight; moreover, his head was a good deal too large. But, on the other hand, his elegant costume showed him to be a person of taste and good upbringing. He had on a very pretty violet cavalry man's jacket, knobs and braid all over, pants

12

of the same, and the loveliest little boots ever seen even on a cavalry officer—fitting his little legs just as if they had been painted on them. He had a little, short cloak on his shoulders, which looked almost as if it were made of wood, and on his head a cap like a miner's. But Marie remembered that Godpapa Drosselmeier often appeared in a terribly ugly jacket, and with a frightful-looking cap on his head, and yet was a very darling godpapa.

As Marie kept looking at this little man, whom she had quite fallen in love with at first sight, she saw more and more clearly what a sweet nature showed on his face. Those green eyes of his beamed with kindness. His chin was set off with a well-kept beard of white cotton, and this drew attention to the smile which his bright red lips always expressed.

"Oh, papa, dear!" cried Marie at last, "whose is that most darling little man beside the tree?"

"Well," was the answer, "that little fellow is going to crack nuts for all of you, and he is to belong to Louise just as much as to you and Fritz." With which papa took him up from the table, and on his lifting the end of the wooden cloak, the little man opened his mouth wider and wider, displaying two rows of very white, sharp teeth. Marie, directed by her father, put a nut into his mouth, and—knack—he had bitten it in two, so that the shells fell down, and Marie got the kernel. So then it was explained to all that this charming little man was a Nutcracker. "And," said papa, "as friend Nutcracker seems to have made such an impression on you, Marie, he shall be given over to your special care, though, as I said, Louise and Fritz are to have the same right to his services as you."

Marie took him into her arms at once, and made him crack some more nuts; but she picked out all the smallest, so that he might not have to open his mouth so terribly wide, because that was not nice for him. Then sister Louise came, and he had to crack some nuts for her, too, which duty he seemed very glad to perform.

Meanwhile, Fritz was a little tired, after so much soldier-play, so he joined his sisters, and laughed beyond measure at the funny little fellow, who (as Fritz wanted his share of the nuts) was passed from hand to hand, and kept snapping his mouth open and shut. Fritz gave him all the biggest and hardest nuts he could find, but all at once there was a "crack— crack," and three teeth fell out of Nutcracker's mouth, and his lower jaw became loose and wobbly.

"Ah! my poor darling Nutcracker," Marie cried, and took him away from Fritz.

"A nice sort of fellow he is!" said Fritz. "Calls himself a nutcracker and can't give a decent bite— doesn't seem to know much about his business. Hand him over here, Marie! I'll keep him biting nuts if he drops all the rest of his teeth, and his jaw, too. What's the good of a fellow like him!"

"No, no," said Marie, in tears; "you shan't have him, my darling Nutcracker; see how he's looking at me so sadly, and showing me his poor sore mouth. You're a hard-hearted creature!"

"But Nutcracker's as much mine as yours," said Fritz, "so hand him over!"

Marie began to cry bitterly, and quickly wrapped the wounded Nutcracker up in her little handkerchief. Papa and mamma came with Drosselmeier, who took

Fritz's side, but papa said, "I have put Nutcracker in Marie's special charge, and as he seems to have need just now of her care, she has full power over him, and nobody else has anything to say in the matter. And

I'm surprised that Fritz should expect further service from a man wounded in the performance of his duty. As a good soldier, he ought to know better than that."

Fritz was much ashamed, and, troubling himself no further as to nuts or nutcrackers, crept off to the other side of the table, where his cavalry men were camping for the night. Marie got Nutcracker's lost teeth together, bound a pretty white ribbon, taken from her dress, about his poor chin, and then wrapped the poor little fellow again in her handkerchief. Thus she held him, rocking him like a child in her arms, as she looked at the picture books. She grew quite angry with Godpapa Drosselmeier because he laughed so, and kept asking how she could make such a fuss about an ugly little fellow like that. That odd likeness it had to Drosselmeier, which had struck her when she saw Nutcracker at first, came to her mind again now, and she said:

"Who knows, godpapa, if you were to be dressed the same as my darling Nutcracker, and had on the same shining boots—who knows whether you mightn't look almost as handsome as he does?"

CHAPTER 4

Wonderful Events

I N THE LIVING-ROOM, on the left hand as you go in, there stands against the wall a high, glass-fronted cupboard, where all the children's Christmas presents are kept. Louise, the elder sister, was still quite little when her father had this cupboard constructed by a skillful workman, who had made it so splendid, that the things, when inside it, looked almost more shining and lovely than when one had them actually in one's hands.

In the upper shelves, which were beyond reach of Fritz and Marie, were stowed Godpapa Drosselmeier's works of art; just under them was the shelf for the picture books. Fritz and Marie were allowed to do what they liked with the two lower shelves, but it always came about that the lowest one of all was where Marie put her dolls, while Fritz used the shelf above this for his troops. On the evening about which we are speaking, Fritz had quartered his cavalry in his—the upper—shelf of these two. Marie had put Miss Gertrude rather in a corner, established the new doll she had just received in the chamber there, with all its furniture, and invited herself to tea and cakes with her. This doll-chamber was splendidly furnished:

a little flowered sofa, a number of charming little chairs, a nice little tea-table, and, above all, a beautiful little white bed, where pretty dolls go to sleep. All this was in a corner of the shelf, the walls of which, in this part, had beautiful little pictures hanging on them; and you may well imagine that the new doll (whose name was Miss Clara) thought herself comfortably settled.

It was getting very late, not so very far from midnight, before the children could tear themselves away from all these Yuletide fascinations, and Godpapa Drosselmeier had been gone a long time. They remained beside the glass cupboard, although their mother several times reminded them that it was long after bedtime. "Yes," said Fritz, "I know well enough that these poor fellows (meaning his cavalry men) are tired enough, and want to turn in for the night, though as long as I'm here, not one of them dares to nod off." But with that, he got up and went to bed. Marie begged for just a little while longer, saying she had such a number of things to see to, and promising that as soon as she had them all settled she would go to bed at once. Marie was a very good and reasonable child, and therefore her mother allowed her to remain a little longer with her toys; but just in case she should be too much occupied with her new doll and other playthings and would forget to put out the candles which were lighted all around on the wall brackets, she herself put all of them out, leaving merely the lamp which hung from the ceiling to give a soft and pleasant light. "Come to bed soon, Marie, or you'll never be up in time in the morning," cried her mother as she went away into the bedroom.

As soon as Marie was alone, she set to work to do what she wanted most to do, which she somehow did not like to set about with her mother there. She had been holding Nutcracker, wrapped in the handkerchief, carefully in her arms all this time, and she now laid him softly down on the table, gently unrolled the handkerchief, and examined his wounds.

"Oh, my darling Nutcracker!" said she, very softly, "don't you be bothered because Fritz has hurt you so. I'll take the greatest care of you, and nurse you, till you're quite, quite better and happy again. And your teeth shall be put in again for you, and your shoulder set right. Godpapa Drosselmeier will see to that; he knows how to do things of that kind."

She took him in her arms, approached the cupboard, and kneeling down beside it, said to her new doll:

"I'm going to ask a favor of you, Miss Clara—that you will give up your bed to this poor sick, wounded Nutcracker, and make yourself as comfortable as you can on the sofa here. Remember that you're well and strong yourself, or you wouldn't have such fat, red cheeks, and that there are very few dolls who have as comfortable a sofa as this to lie upon."

Marie took the bed and moved it forward; laid Nutcracker carefully and tenderly down on it; wrapped another pretty ribbon taken from her own dress about his hurt shoulder, and drew the bedclothes up to his nose. Then she moved the bed, with Nutcracker in it, to the upper shelf, so that it was placed near the village in which Fritz's cavalry men had their sleeping quarters. She closed the cupboard, and was moving away to go to bed, when—listen, children!—there began a low soft rustling and rattling, and a sort of whispering noise, all round, in all directions, from all sides of the room—behind the stove, under the chairs, behind the cupboards.

The clock on the wall "warned" louder and louder, but could not strike. Marie looked at it, and saw that the big gold-painted owl which was on the top of it had drooped its wings so that they covered the whole of the clock, and had stretched its catlike head, with the crooked beak, a long way forward. And the "warning" kept growing louder and louder, with distinct words: "Clocks, clocks, stop ticking. No sound, but cautious 'warning.' Mouse-King's ears are fine. Prr-prr. Only sing poom, poom; sing the olden song of doom! prr-prr; poom, poom. Bells go chime! Soon rings out

the deadly time!" And then came a low "Poom! poom!" twelve times.

Marie grew terribly frightened, and was going to rush away, when she noticed that Godpapa Drosselmeier was up on the top of the clock instead of the owl, with his yellow coattails hanging down on both sides like wings. She called out in a loud voice:

"Godpapa! godpapa! what are you up there for? Come down to me, and don't frighten me so terribly, you naughty, naughty Godpapa Drosselmeier!"

But then there began a sort of wild kickering and squeaking, everywhere, all about, and soon there was the sound of running, as of thousands of little feet behind the walls, and thousands of little lights began to glitter out between the chinks of the woodwork. But they were not lights; no, no! They were little glittering eyes; and Marie became aware that, everywhere, mice were peeping and squeezing themselves out through every chink. Soon they were trotting and galloping in all directions over the room.

As Marie was not afraid of mice, she could not help being amused by this, and her first alarm had nearly left her, when suddenly there came a sharp and terrible piping noise. Ah! what did she see then?

Seven mouse-heads, with seven shining crowns upon them rose through the floor, hissing and piping in a most horrible way. Quickly the body of the mouse which had these seven crowned heads forced its way up through the floor. This enormous creature shouted, with its seven heads, aloud to the crowd of mice, squeaking to them with all the seven mouths at the same time. Then the entire army set itself in motion, and went trot, trot, right up to the cupboard—and, in fact, to Marie, who was standing beside it.

Half-fainting, Marie leant backwards, and then there was a "klirr, klirr, prr," and a pane of the cupboard, broken by her elbow, fell in shivers to the floor. She felt for a moment the sharp, stinging pain in her arms, and then everything was quiet; and though she didn't dare to look, she thought the noise of the breaking glass had frightened the mice back to their holes.

But what happened next? Right behind Marie a movement seemed to start in the cupboard, and small, faint voices began to be heard, saying:

> Out to the fight, out to the fight;
> Arm yourselves, this is the night.

And bells began ringing prettily.

"Oh! those are my bells!" cried Marie, and went nearer and looked in. Then she saw that there was bright light in the cupboard; dolls and little figures of various kinds all running about together, and struggling with their little weapons. At this point, Nutcracker rose from his bed, cast off the blankets, and sprang with both feet onto the floor (of the shelf), crying out at the top of his voice:

Knack, knack, knack,
Stupid mousey pack,
All their skulls we'll crack.
Mousey pack, mousey pack,
Knick, knack, crick and crack,
Come, men, force them back!

And with this he drew his little sword, waved it in the air, and cried:

"My trusty men, brothers, and friends, are you ready to stand by me in this great battle?"

Immediately three wobbly-kneed cowards, one creaky old man, four chimney-sweeps, two guitar players, and a drummer cried:

"Yes, your highness; we will stand by you in loyal duty; we will follow you to the fight!" And they tumbled after Nutcracker (who, in the excitement of the moment, had dared to leap down) to the bottom shelf. Now *they* might well dare this leap, for not only had they got plenty of clothes on, of cloth and silk, but besides, there was not much in their insides except cotton and sawdust, so that they plumped down like little wool-sacks. But as for poor Nutcracker, he would certainly have broken his arms and legs; for, remember, it was nearly two feet from where he had stood to the shelf below, and his body was as brittle as if he had been made of hard candy. Yes, Nutcracker would have broken his arms and legs, had not Miss Clara started up at the moment of his spring, and caught the hero in her tender arms.

He at once sank gracefully on one knee, and said:

"Oh, lady! I will always remember the kind help you have given me!"

At this, he waved his glittering sword, and sprang like a bird over the ledge of the cupboard down to the floor.

CHAPTER 5

The Battle

"BEAT THE MARCH, trusty drummer!" cried Nutcracker, and immediately the drummer began to roll his drum in the most splendid style, so that the windows of the glass cupboard rattled and resounded. Then there began a cracking and clattering inside, and Marie saw all the lids of the boxes in which Fritz's army was quartered bursting open. The soldiers all came out and jumped down to the bottom shelf, where they formed up in good order. Nutcracker hurried up and down the ranks, speaking words of encouragement.

Then there began a tramping and a neighing in the cupboard; and Fritz's toy soldiers—but above all, the new glittering cavalry—marched out, and then came to a halt, drawn up on the floor. They then marched past Nutcracker by regiments, with flags flying and bands playing. After this they wheeled into line, and formed up at right angles to the line of march. Upon this, Fritz's artillery came rattling up, and formed in advance of the halted cavalry. Then it went "boom-boom!" and Marie saw the sugar-plums bombing down upon the thickly-massed mouse-battalions, which were powdered quite white by them. But a battery of heavy guns, which had taken up a strong position on mamma's footstool, was what did the greatest damage; and "poom-poom-poom!" kept up a fire of gingerbread nuts into the enemy's ranks, mowing the mice down in great numbers.

The enemy, however, was not much checked in its advance, and had even got hold itself of one or two of the heavy guns, when there came "prr-prr-prr!" and Marie could scarcely see what was happening for smoke and dust; but this much is certain, that every unit of men fought with the utmost bravery and determination, and it was for a long time doubtful which side would win. The mice kept on bringing new fighters to their forces, as they moved toward the scene of action; their little silver cannon balls—like pills in size—they aimed with great skill and even shot into the glass cupboard. Clara and Gertrude, the dolls, ran up and down in fright, and loudly crying.

"Must I—the very loveliest doll in the world—die in the very flower of my youth?" cried Miss Clara.

"Oh! was it for this," wept Gertrude, "that I have taken such pains to keep my looks all these years? Must I be shot here in my own living-room, after all?"

They fell into each other's arms, and howled so terribly that you could hear them above the noise of the battle. The battle sounds went prr-prr-poof, piff-schneyer-ding—ping-josh—schneyer-ding—boom-booroom—boom-booroom—boom—all now and then and here and everywhere. And the mouse-king and the mice squeaked and screamed; and then again

Nutcracker's powerful voice was heard shouting words of command, and issuing important orders, and he was seen striding along amongst his battalions in the thick of the fire.

During the hottest part of the fight, masses of mouse cavalry had been quietly popping out from the chest of drawers, and had then made an advance upon the left wing of Nutcracker's force, uttering loud and horrible squeakings. But what a force they met with! The regiment of figures commanded by two Chinese emperors advanced. These fine, brilliantly uniformed troops, consisting of gardeners, Tyrolese, Siberians, hairdressers, clowns, Cupids, lions, tigers, unicorns, and monkeys, fought with the utmost courage.

This battalion would have seized the victory from the enemy had not one of the mouse cavalry captains made a charge upon one of the Chinese emperors and bitten off his head. The emperor, in his fall, knocked over and smotherd a couple of Siberians and a unicorn, and this created a gap through which the enemy charged, which resulted in the whole battalion being bitten to death. But the enemy gained little advantage by this; for as soon as one of the mouse-cavalry soldiers bit one of these brave figures to death, he found that there was a small piece of printed paper (each of the toys bore a label from its maker) sticking in his throat, of which he died in a moment. Still, this was of small advantage to Nutcracker's army, which, having once started to retreat, went on farther and farther, suffering greater and greater losses. The unlucky Nutcracker soon found himself driven back close to the front of the cupboard, with a very small portion of his army.

"Bring up the reserves! Old man! Clowns! Drummer! Where the devil have you got to?" shouted Nutcracker, who was still counting on more troops from the cupboard. And there did, in fact, advance a small group of brown gingerbread men and women, with golden faces, hats, and helmets; but they waddled so clumsily that they never hit any of the enemy, and soon knocked off the cap of their commander-in-chief, Nutcracker himself. And the enemy's foot soldiers soon bit their legs off, so that they tumbled topsy-turvy, jervey-tervy, and killed several of Nutcracker's companions at the same time.

Nutcracker was now hard pressed, and closely hemmed in by the enemy, and in a position of danger. He tried to jump to the bottom ledge of the cupboard, but his legs were not long enough. Clara and Gertrude had fainted; so they could give no help. Cavalry men came charging up at him, and he shouted:

"A horse! a horse! My kingdom for a horse!"

At this moment two of the enemy's riflemen seized him by his wooden cloak, and the king of the mice went rushing up at him, squeaking in triumph out of all his seven throats.

Marie could contain herself no longer. "Oh! my poor Nutcracker!" she sobbed, took her left shoe off, and threw it as hard as she could into the thick of the enemy, straight at their king.

Instantly everything vanished! All was silence. But Marie felt a more stinging pain than before in her left arm, and fell on the floor in a faint.

CHAPTER 6

The Invalid

WHEN MARIE AWOKE from a deep sleep she was lying in her little bed; and the sun was shining brightly in at the window, which was all covered with frost-flowers. There was a strange gentleman sitting beside her, whom she recognized as Dr. Wendelstern. "She's awake," he said softly, and her mother came and looked at her with great concern.

"Oh, mother!" whispered Marie, "are all those horrid mice gone away, and is Nutcracker quite safe?"

"Don't talk such nonsense, Marie," answered her mother. "What have the mice to do with Nutcracker? You're a very naughty girl, and have caused us all a great deal of worry. See what comes of children not doing as they're told! You were playing with your toys so late last night that you fell asleep. I don't know whether or not some mouse jumped out and frightened you, though there are no mice here, generally. But you broke a pane of the glass cupboard with your elbow, and cut your arm so badly that Dr. Wendelstern (who has just taken a number of pieces of glass out of your arm) thinks that if it had been a little higher up you might have had a stiff arm for life, or even have bled to death. Thank Heaven, I awoke

31

about twelve o'clock and missed you; and I found you fainted in front of the glass cupboard, bleeding frightfully, with a number of Fritz's soldiers scattered round you, and Nutcracker was lying on your bleeding arm, with your left shoe not far off."

"Oh, mother, mother," said Marie, "these were the remains of the tremendous battle between the toys and the mice; and what frightened me was that the mice were going to take Nutcracker prisoner. Then I threw my shoe in among the mice, and after that I know nothing more that happened."

Dr. Wendelstern gave a meaningful look to her mother, who said very gently to Marie:

"Never mind, dear, keep yourself quiet. The mice are all gone away, and Nutcracker's in the cupboard, quite safe and sound."

Here Marie's father came in, and had a long talk with Dr. Wendelstern. Then he felt Marie's pulse, and she heard them talking about "wound-fever." She had to stay in bed and take medicine for several days, because her arm was rather stiff and painful. These days seemed very long to her, and she could scarcely pass the time till evening, when her mother came and sat at her bedside, telling her a story. One evening the door opened and in came Godpapa Drosselmeier, saying:

"I've come to see with my own eyes how Marie's getting on."

When Marie saw Godpapa Drosselmeier in his little yellow coat, the scene of the night when Nutcracker lost the battle with the mice came so clearly back to her that she couldn't help crying out:

"Oh! Godpapa Drosselmeier, how nasty you were! I saw you quite well when you were sitting on the clock, covering it all over with your wings to prevent it from striking and frightening the mice. I heard you quite well when you called the Mouse-King. Why didn't you help Nutcracker? Why didn't you help *me*, you nasty godpapa? It's nobody's fault but yours that I'm lying here with a bad arm."

Her mother, in much alarm, asked what she meant. But Drosselmeier began making faces, and said, in a snarling voice, like a sort of chant:

"Pendulums could only rattle—couldn't tick, never a click; all the clocks stopped their ticking: no more clicking; then they all struck loud, cling-clang. Hink and hank, and honk and hank. Cling and ring! The battle's over—Nutcracker all safe in clover. Comes the owl, on downy wing—scares away the mouses' king! Pendulums must click again!"

Marie fixed wide eyes of terror upon Godpapa Drosselmeier, because he was jerking his right arm backwards and forwards as if he were some puppet moved by a handle. Fritz (who had just arrived) laughed, saying, "Why, godpapa, you *are* funny!"

But their mother looked very grave, and said, "This is a most odd way of going on, Mr. Drosselmeier. What can you mean by it?"

"My goodness!" said Drosselmeier, laughing, "did you never hear my nice Watchmaker's Song? I always sing it to little invalids like Marie." Then he sat down beside Marie's bed, and said to her, "Don't be angry with me because I didn't poke out all the Mouse-King's fourteen eyes. That couldn't be managed exactly; but to make up for it, here's something which I know will please you."

He dived into one of his pockets, and what he slowly, slowly brought out of it was—Nutcracker! whose teeth he had put in again quite firmly, and set his broken jaw completely. Marie shouted for joy, and her mother laughed and said, "Now you see for yourself how nice Godpapa Drosselmeier is to Nut-cracker."

"But you must admit, Marie," said her godpapa, "that Nutcracker is far from being what you might call a handsome fellow. If you like, I'll tell you how it was that the ugliness came into his family, and has been handed down in it from one generation to another. Did you ever hear about the Princess Pirlipat, the witch Mouserink, and the clever Clockmaker?"

"I say, Godpapa Drosselmeier," interrupted Fritz, "you've put Nutcracker's teeth in again all right, and his jaw isn't wobbly as it was; but what's become of his sword? Why haven't you given him a sword?"

"Oh," cried Drosselmeier, annoyed, "you must always be bothering and finding fault with something or other, boy. What do I have to do with Nutcracker's sword? I've fixed his mouth for him; he must look out for a sword for himself."

"Yes, yes," said Fritz, "so he must."

"So tell me, Marie," continued Drosselmeier, "if you know the story of Princess Pirlipat?"

"Oh, no," said Marie. "Tell it to me, please!"

"I hope it won't be as strange and terrible as your stories generally are," said her mother.

"Oh, no, nothing of the kind," said Drosselmeier. "On the contrary, it's quite a funny story which I'm going to have the honor of telling this time."

"Go on, then—tell it to us!" cried the children; and Drosselmeier began as follows:——

CHAPTER 7

The Story of the Hard Nut

PIRLIPAT'S MOTHER WAS a king's wife, so that, of course, she was a queen; and Pirlipat herself was a princess by birth as soon as she was born. The king was beside himself with joy over his beautiful little daughter as she lay in her cradle, and he danced round and round upon one leg, crying again and again:

"Hurrah! hurrah! Hip, hip, hurray! Did anybody ever see anything so lovely as my little Pirlipat?"

And all the ministers of state, and the generals, the senators, and the officers of the staff, danced about on one leg, as the king did, and cried as loud as they could, "No, no—never!"

Indeed, no one could say that a lovelier baby than Princess Pirlipat had ever been born since the world began. Her little face looked as if it were woven of the most delicate white and rose-colored silk; her eyes were of sparkling blue, and her hair all in little curls like threads of gold. Moreover, she had come into the world with two rows of little pearly teeth, with which, two hours after her birth, she bit the Lord High Chancellor in the fingers when he was making a careful examination of her features, so that he cried, "Oh! Gemini!" quite loudly.

All was joy and gladness, as I have said, except that the queen was very worried and uneasy, nobody could tell why. She had Pirlipat's cradle most carefully guarded. Not only were there always guards at the doors of the nursery, but—over and beyond the two head nurses close to the cradle—there always had to be six other nurses all around the room at night. And what seemed rather a funny thing, which nobody could understand, was that each of these six nurses always had to have a cat in her lap, and to keep on stroking it all night long, so that it would never stop purring.

It is impossible that you, my reader, should know the reason of all these measures; but I do, and shall tell you why they were so.

Once upon a time, many great kings and very grand princes were gathered at Pirlipat's father's court, and very great doings were in the works. Tournaments, plays and dances were going on, and the king, to show that he had no lack of gold and silver, made up his mind to make a good show of it all. He decided to give a grand pudding-and-sausage banquet. He jumped into a state carriage, and personally invited all the kings and the princes from surrounding lands. On his return he said to the queen, very kindly, "My darling, *you* know exactly how I like my puddings and sausages!"

The queen quite understood what this meant. It meant that she should undertake the important duty of making the puddings and sausages herself. So she got out the great golden sausage kettle, and the silver casseroles. A great fire was kindled, the queen put on

her apron, and soon the most delicious aroma of pudding broth rose steaming out of the kettle. This sweet smell spread into the very council chamber. The king could not control himself.

"Excuse me for a few minutes, my lords and gentlemen," he cried; then he rushed to the kitchen, hugged the queen, stirred the kettle a little with his golden sceptre, and then went back to the council chamber.

The important moment had now arrived when the fat had to be cut up into little square pieces, and browned on silver spits. The ladies-in-waiting went away now, because the queen thought it proper to perform this important task alone. But when the fat began to brown, a little whisper made itself heard, saying, "Give me some of that, sister! I want some of it, too; I am a queen as well as yourself; give me some."

The queen knew well who was speaking. It was Dame Mouserink, who had lived in the palace for many years. She claimed kinship with the royal family, and she was queen of Mousolia herself, and lived with a large following of her own under the kitchen hearth. The queen was kind-hearted; she was willing, at this festive season, to spare her the tidbits she asked for. So she said, "Come out, then, Dame Mouserink; of course you shall taste my browned fat."

So Dame Mouserink came running out as fast as she could, held up her pretty little paws, and took morsel after morsel of the browned fat as the queen held them out to her. But then all Dame Mouserink's uncles, and her cousins, and her aunts, came jumping out too; and her seven sons (who were terrible nogoods) as well; and they all went at the browned fat, and the queen was too frightened to keep them off.

Most fortunately the mistress of the robes came in, and drove these rude visitors away, so that a little of the browned fat was left; and then, it was found possible, by careful measurement, to divvy up the fat among the sausages under construction.

The kettledrums and the trumpets summoned all the great princes and kings to the feast. They came in their formal robes. The king received them with much ceremony, and took his seat at the head of the table, with his crown on, and his sceptre in his hand. Even during the serving of the white pudding course, it was observed that he turned pale, and raised his eyes to heaven; sighs heaved his chest. When the black puddings were handed round, he fell back in his seat, loudly sobbing and groaning.

Everyone rose from the table, and the court doctor tried to feel his pulse. Finally, after the doctor gave him various doses of remedies, His Majesty seemed to recover his senses, and stammered the words: "Too little fat!"

The queen cast herself down at his feet in despair, and cried, in a voice broken by sobs, "Oh, my poor royal husband! Ah, what tortures you must feel! Alas! Dame Mouserink, her uncles, her seven sons, her cousins and her aunts, came and ate up nearly all the fat—and——"

Here the queen fell back in a faint.

The king jumped up, and cried, "Mistress of the robes, what is the meaning of this?"

The mistress of the robes told all she knew, and the king decided to take revenge on Dame Mouserink and her family for eating up the fat which ought to have been in the sausages. His councillors were summoned, and they decided that Dame Mouserink should be punished, and all her property taken away. He called upon the court clockmaker and inventor—whose name was the same as mine—Christian Elias Drosselmeier, and he undertook to get rid of Dame Mouserink and all her relations from the palace forever. He invented little machines, into which pieces of browned fat were inserted; and he placed these machines down all about the dwelling of Dame Mouserink. Now she herself was much too clever not to see through Drosselmeier's trick; but all her warnings to her relatives failed to stop them from falling prey to the machines. Tempted by the fragrant odor of the browned fat, all her seven sons, and a great many of her uncles, cousins, and aunts, walked into Drosselmeier's little machines and were immediately taken prisoner by the fall of a small gate, after which they met their death in the kitchen.

Dame Mouserink left this scene of horror with her small following. Rage and despair filled her. The court rejoiced; the queen, however, was very worried, because she knew Dame Mouserink's character, and knew well that she would never allow the death of her sons and other relatives to go unavenged. And, in fact, one day when the queen was cooking lamb for the king, Dame Mouserink suddenly made her appearance, and said: "My sons and my uncles, my cousins and my aunts, are now no more. Be careful, queen, or I will bite your little princess in two! This is my warning!"

The queen was so frightened that she dropped the dish she was preparing into the fire.

And now you know, children, why it was the queen took such precautions about her little Pirlipat. Had she not always the fear before her eyes of Dame Mouserink coming back and carrying out her threat of biting the princess to death? Drosselmeier's clever machines were of no use against the crafty Dame Mouserink, and nobody except the court astronomer, who was also the state astrologer and reader of the stars, knew that the family of the Cat Purr had the power to keep her away. This was why each of the nurses had to keep one of the Cat Purr's sons in her lap.

One night, just after midnight, one of the chief nurses woke suddenly from a deep sleep. Everything lay buried in slumber. Not a purr was to be heard. What were the feelings of this nurse when she saw, close beside her, a great, hideous mouse, standing on its hind legs, with its horrid head laid on the princess's face. She sprang up with a scream of terror. Everybody awoke; but then Dame Mouserink (for she was the great big mouse in Pirlipat's cradle) ran quickly away into the corner of the room. The king's councillors dashed after her, but too late! She was off and away through a chink in the floor. The noise awoke Pirlipat, who cried terribly. "Heaven be thanked she is still alive!" shouted all the nurses; but what was their horror when they looked at Pirlipat, and saw what the beautiful, fine little thing had turned into. A great big swollen head (instead of the pretty little golden-haired one) at the top of a tiny, crumpled-up body, and green, wooden-looking eyes staring where the lovely blue pair had been, while her mouth had stretched across from the one ear to the other.

Of course the queen nearly died of weeping, and the walls of the king's study all had to be padded, because he kept banging his head against them, crying:

"Oh, what a miserable king am I! Oh, what a miserable king am I!"

He might have seen then, that it would have been much better to eat his puddings with no fat in them at all, and let Dame Mouserink and her folk stay on under the hearthstone. But Pirlipat's royal father did not think of that. What he did was to lay all the blame on the court clockmaker and inventor, Christian Elias Drosselmeier, of Nuremberg. So he ordered that Drosselmeier should within the space of four weeks restore Princess Pirlipat to her former, beautiful condition or else be put to death.

Drosselmeier was quite alarmed. He saw that the bigger she grew the more deformed she would be, and so he didn't know what was to be done at all. He scratched his head and sank down beside the cradle— which he wasn't allowed to go away from.

It was Wednesday of the fourth week when the king came in with eyes gleaming with anger, made threatening gestures with his sceptre, and said:

"Christian Elias Drosselmeier, restore the princess, or prepare to die!"

Drosselmeier began to weep. The little princess kept on cracking nuts, something which she seemed to enjoy. For the first time the inventor was struck by Pirlipat's remarkable appetite for nuts, and the fact that she had been born with teeth. And immediately after her change into an ugly creature she had begun to cry, and she had gone on crying till by chance she had got hold of a nut. She at once cracked it, and ate the kernel, after which she was quite quiet. From that time the nurses found that nothing would do but to go on giving her nuts.

"Oh, holy Nature!" cried Drosselmeier. "You have pointed out to me the door of the secret. I will knock, and it shall be opened to me!"

He at once begged to be able to consult with the court astronomer, and was led to him closely guarded. They embraced with many tears, for they were great friends, and then went into a small room where they referred to many books on mysterious subjects. Night came on. The court astronomer looked at the stars, and with the assistance of Drosselmeier discovered the princess's horoscope. It lay plain before them that all the princess had to do to be delivered from the enchantment which made her so hideous and get back to her former beauty was to eat the sweet kernel of the nut Crackatook.

Now this nut Crackatook had a shell so hard that you might have fired a cannon ball at it without giving it a scratch. Moreover, this nut should be cracked, in the princess's presence, by the teeth of a man whose beard had never been shaved, and who had never had on boots. This man had to hand the kernel to her with his eyes closed, and he might not open them till he had made seven steps backward without a stumble.

Drosselmeier and the astronomer had been at work on this problem for three days and three nights; and on the following Saturday the king was sitting at dinner when Drosselmeier—who was to have been beheaded on the Sunday morning—burst in joyfully to announce that he had found out what had to be done to restore Princess Pirlipat to her former beauty. The king hugged him, and promised him a diamond sword, four medals and two Sunday suits once this was done.

Drosselmeier stammered out that though the remedy was discovered, both the nut Crackatook and the young gentleman who was to crack it had still to be searched for, and that it was a matter of doubt whether they ever would be found at all. The king, becoming angry, announced that Drosselmeier and the astronomer should start off immediately, and not come back without the nut Crackatook in their pockets. The man who was to crack it (by the queen's suggestion) might be heard of by means of advertisements in the local and foreign newspapers and magazines.

Drosselmeier and the court astronomer had been journeying for fifteen long years without finding the slightest trace of the nut Crackatook. It was in Nuremberg, Drosselmeier's hometown, that the clockmaker went to his cousin the toymaker and doll-carver, whom he had not seen for a great many long years. To him he told all the tale of Princess Pirlipat, Dame Mouserink and the nut Crackatook, so that his cousin clapped his hands and cried in amazement:

"Dear me, cousin, these things are really wonderful—very wonderful, indeed!"

Drosselmeier told him, further, some of the adventures he had met with on his long journey; how he had been everywhere utterly unsuccessful in discovering the faintest trace of the nut Crackatook. During this story, Christoph Zacharias, his cousin, had kept snapping his fingers, twisting himself round on one foot and smacking his lips; then he cried:

"Oh!—that really would be something!"

At last he threw his hat and wig in the air, warmly hugged his cousin, and cried:

"Cousin, cousin, you've done it!—for either I am much mistaken, or I have the nut Crackatook myself!"

He immediately brought out a little cardboard box, out of which he took a gold-coated nut of medium size.

"Look there!" he said. "Several years ago at Christmas a stranger came here with a sack of nuts, which he offered for sale. Just in front of my shop he got into a fight, and put the sack down the better to defend himself from the local nutsellers, who attacked him. Just then a loaded wagon drove over the sack, and all the nuts were smashed except one. The stranger offered to sell me this nut for twenty kreuzers. I found such a coin in my pocket, so I bought the nut, and I gold-coated it, though I didn't know why I took the trouble, or should have paid so much for it."

All question as to its being really the long-looked for nut Crackatook disappeared when the court astronomer carefully scraped away the gold coating, and found the word "Crackatook" engraved on the shell in Chinese letters.

Their joy was great, as you may imagine.

The astronomer told the inventor:

"One piece of good fortune never comes alone. I feel convinced that we've not only found the nut, but the young gentleman who is to crack it, and hand the beauty-restoring kernel to the princess, as well. I mean none other than your cousin's son here."

The cousin's son was a nice-looking, well-grown young fellow, had never been shaved, and had never worn boots. He had appeared last Christmas in a beautiful red coat with gold trimmings, a sword by his side, his hat under his arm, and a fine wig with a pigtail. Thus outfitted, he stood in his father's shop lovely to behold, and out of politeness he took to cracking nuts for the young ladies, who called him "the handsome nutcracker."

"This is the very man!" cried the astronomer. "We have him! He is found! Only, dearest partner, we must make a strong and heavy pigtail for this nephew of yours, which shall be connected with his lower jaw in such a way that it shall be capable of giving a very powerful pull. And next, when we get back to the king, we must carefully hide the fact that we have brought the young gentleman who is to crack the nut back with us. He must not make his appearance for a while. I read in his horoscope that if two or three others bite at the nut unsuccessfully to begin with, the king will promise the man who breaks it—and restores her good looks to the princess—the princess's hand in marriage and the future kingship."

The doll-maker cousin was delighted with the idea of his son's marrying Princess Pirlipat and being a prince and king, so he gave him over to his cousin to do what he liked with him. The pigtail which Drosselmeier attached to him proved to be powerful, as he showed by cracking the hardest of peach-stones with ease.

Drosselmeier and the astronomer, having sent news to the king of the discovery of the nut Crackatook, the necessary advertisements were at once put in the newspapers, and by the time that the travellers got there, several nice young gentlemen had arrived, among whom there were even princes, who had enough confidence in their teeth to try to restore the princess. The clockmaker and astronomer were horrified when they saw poor Pirlipat again. The little body with tiny hands and feet was not big enough to support the big, shapeless head. The hideousness of the face was worse, with its beard like white cotton, which had grown about the mouth and chin. Everything turned out as the court astronomer predicted. One fool after another bit his teeth and jaws into painful agonies over the nut without doing the princess the slightest good in the world. Then he would sigh:

"Ah dear, that *was* a hard nut."

Finally, when the king promised that whoever disenchanted Pirlipat would have the kingdom and the princess, the charming, gentle young Drosselmeier made his appearance, and begged to be allowed to make an attempt. None of the previous nut-biters had pleased the princess so much. She pressed her little hands to her heart and sighed:

"Ah, I hope it will be he who will crack the nut and be my husband."

When he had politely saluted the king, the queen and the Princess Pirlipat, he received the nut Cracka-took from the hands of a clerk, put it between his teeth, made a strong effort with his head, and—crack—crack—the shell was shattered into a number of pieces. He neatly cleared the kernel from the pieces of husk which were sticking to it, and bending on one knee, presented it to the princess, after which he closed his eyes and began his backward steps. The princess swallowed the kernel, and—oh!—the monster vanished, and in its place there stood a wonderfully beautiful lady with a face which seemed woven of lily-white and rose-red silk, eyes of sparkling blue and hair all in little curls like threads of gold.

Trumpets and kettledrums mingled in the loud rejoicings of the people. The king and all his court danced about on one leg, as they had done at Pirlipat's birth, and the queen had to be revived from a fainting fit of joy and delight. All this tremendous celebration got in the way of young Drosselmeier's concentration, for he still had to make his seven backward steps. Just as he was stretching out his right foot to make his seventh step, up came Dame Mouserink through the floor, making a horrible squeaking, so that Drosselmeier, as he was putting his foot down, stepped upon her and stumbled so that he almost fell. Oh misery!—all in an instant he was transformed, just as the princess had been before: his body all shrivelled up, and could scarcely support the great shapeless head with big eyes and the wide gaping mouth. In the place where his pigtail used to be was a wooden cloak which controlled the movements of his lower jaw.

The clockmaker and the astronomer were wild with terror, but they saw that Dame Mouserink was lying in her own blood on the floor. Her wickedness had not escaped punishment, for young Drosselmeier had squashed her with the sharp point of his shoe.

But as Dame Mouserink lay there dying she squeaked and cheeped sadly and cried:

"Oh, Crackatook, you hard nut!—Hee hee, tee tee, woe is me!—Because of that hard nut I must die.—But brave young Nutcracker, I see—you soon must follow after me.—My sweet young son, with seven heads and seven crowns—will soon bring Master Nutcracker down.—His mother's death he will repay—so, Nutcracker, beware that day!—Oh, sweet life, I say goodbye—I leave you now, for I must die. Queak!"

With this cry died Dame Mouserink, and her body was carried out. Meantime, nobody had been troubling himself about young Drosselmeier. But the princess reminded the king of his promise, and he at once ordered that the young hero be brought to him. But when the poor wretch came forward in his changed condition the princess put both her hands to her face, and cried:

"Oh, please take away that horrid Nutcracker!"

A lord seized him immediately by his little shoulders, and tossed him out the door. The king, angry at the idea of a nutcracker being brought before him as a son-in-law, laid all the blame upon the clockmaker and the astronomer, and ordered them both to be banished from the country forever.

The horoscope which the astronomer had drawn in Nuremberg had said nothing about this; but that didn't stop him from taking some fresh observations. And the stars told him that young Drosselmeier would behave so well in his new condition that he would still be a prince and a king, in spite of his transformation; but also that his deformity would only disappear after the son of Dame Mouserink, the seven-headed king of the mice (whom she had borne after the death of her original seven sons) should die by his hand, and a lady should fall in love with him, even with his deformity.

That is the story of the hard nut, children, and now you know why people so often use the expression "that was a hard nut to crack," and why nutcrackers are so ugly.

And with that, Godpapa Drosselmeier finished his tale.

Chapter 8

Uncle and Nephew

SHOULD ANY OF my readers or listeners ever have happened to be cut by glass they will know what a nasty thing it is, and how long it takes to heal. Marie had to stay in bed a whole week because she felt so terribly dizzy whenever she tried to stand up; but at last she was quite well again, and able to jump about as before. Things in the glass cupboard looked very fine indeed—everything new and shiny, trees and flowers and houses—toys of every kind. Above all, Marie found her dear Nutcracker again, smiling at her in the second shelf, with his teeth all sound and right.

As she looked at this pet of hers, it suddenly struck her that all Godpapa Drosselmeier's story had been about Nutcracker, and his family feud with Dame Mouserink and her people. And now she knew that her Nutcracker was none other than young Mr. Drosselmeier, of Nuremberg, Godpapa Drosselmeier's delightful nephew, unfortunately under the spell of Dame Mouserink. For while the story was being told, Marie couldn't doubt for a moment that the clever clockmaker at Pirlipat's father's court was Godpapa Drosselmeier himself.

"But why didn't your uncle help you? Why didn't he help you?" cried Marie. "Though you're not able to move, or to say a word to me, dear Mr. Drosselmeier, I know you understand me and see how very well I wish you. Always count on my help when you need it."

Twilight came on. Marie's father came in with Godpapa Drosselmeier, and soon Louise set out the tea-table, and the family took their places around it, talking pleasantly and merrily. Marie had sat down at her godpapa's feet in silence. When everybody happened to stop talking at the same time, Marie looked her godpapa full in the face with her great blue eyes, and said:

"I know now, godpapa, that my Nutcracker is your nephew, young Mr. Drosselmeier from Nuremberg. The prediction has come true: he is a king and a prince just as your friend the astronomer said he would be. But you know as well as I do that he is at war with Dame Mouserink's son—that horrid king of the mice. Why don't you help him?"

Marie told the whole story of the battle, as she had witnessed it, and was often interrupted by the loud laughter of her mother and sister; but Fritz and Drosselmeier listened quite closely.

"Where in the name of goodness has the child got her head filled with all that nonsense?" cried her father.

"She has such a lively imagination, you see," said her mother; "she dreamt it all when she was feverish with her arm."

"It is all nonsense," cried Fritz, "and it isn't true!"

But godpapa smiled strangely, and took little Marie on his knee, speaking more gently to her than ever he had been known to do before.

"More is given to you, Marie dear," he said, "than to me, or the others. You are a born princess, like Pirlipat, and you rule over a bright beautiful country. But you still have much to suffer, if you mean to make friends with my poor transformed Nutcracker; for the king of the mice lies in wait for him at every turn. But I cannot help him; you, and you alone, can do that. So be faithful and true."

CHAPTER 9

Victory

I T WAS NOT very long before Marie was awakened one
bright moonlit night by a strange noise which
came from one of the corners of her room. There was
a sound of small stones being thrown, and rolled
here and there; and every so often there came a
horrid cheeping and squeaking.

"Oh, dear me! here come these terrible mice again!"
cried Marie in terror, and she wanted to awaken her
mother. But the noise suddenly stopped; and she
could not move a muscle—for she saw the king of
the mice working himself out through a hole in the
wall. At last he came into the room, ran around in it,
and got onto the little table at the head of her bed
with a great jump.

"Hee-hehee!" he cried; "give me your candy! Out with your cakes, marzipan and sugar-sticks, gingerbread cakes! Don't argue! If you won't give them up, I'll chew up Nutcracker! Just see if I don't!"

As he cried out these terrible words, he chattered his teeth most frightfully, and then made off again through the hole in the wall. This frightened Marie and she was quite pale in the morning, and so upset that she scarcely could utter a word. A hundred times she felt she must go and tell her mother or her sister, or even her brother, what had happened. But she thought, "Of course none of them would believe me. They would only laugh at me."

But she saw well enough that to help Nutcracker she would have to sacrifice all her sweet things; so she laid out all she had of them at the bottom of her cupboard the next evening.

"I can't make out how the mice have got into the living-room," said her mother. "This is something quite new. There never were any there before. See, Marie, they've eaten up all your candy."

And so it was: the Mouse-King hadn't found the marzipan very tasty, and had gnawed all round the edges of it, so that what he had left of it had to be thrown out with the garbage. But Marie did not mind about her candy, pleased to think that she had saved Nutcracker by means of it. But what were her feelings when the next night there again came a squeaking close by her ear. Alas! The king of the mice was there again, with his eyes glaring worse than the night before.

"Give me your sugar toys," he cried; "give them you must, or else I'll chew Nutcracker up into dust!"

Then he was gone again.

Marie was very sorry. She had a beautiful collection of sugar toys. Not only had she a charming little shepherd, with his shepherdess, looking after a flock of milk-white sheep, with a nice dog jumping about them, but two postmen with letters in their hands, and four couples of young gentlemen and beautifully dressed young ladies, swinging in a Russian swing. Then there were two or three dancers, and behind them Farmer Feldkuemmel and the Maid of Orleans. Marie didn't much care about *them;* but back in the corner there was a little baby with red cheeks, and this was Marie's darling. Tears came to her eyes.

"Ah!" she cried, turning to Nutcracker, "I really will do all I can to help you. But it's very hard."

Nutcracker looked at her so miserably that she decided to sacrifice everything—for she remembered the Mouse-King with all his seven mouths wide open to swallow the poor fellow; so that night she set down all her sugar figures in front of the cupboard, as she had the candy the night before. She kissed the shepherd, the shepherdess, and the lambs; and at last she brought her best beloved of all, the little red-cheeked baby from its corner, but did put it a little further back than the rest. Farmer Feldkuemmel and the Maid of Orleans had to stand in front.

"This is really getting too bad," said Marie's mother the next morning; "some nasty mouse or other must

have made a hole in the glass cupboard, for poor Marie's sugar figures are all eaten and gnawed."

In the evening Marie's mother was telling her father and Godpapa Drosselmeier about the trouble some mouse was doing in the children's cupboard, and her father said:

"What a pest! What a pity that we can't get rid of it. It's destroying all the poor child's things."

Ah, how did it go with Marie that night? Something as cold as ice went skittering up her arms, and something rough and nasty spread itself over her cheek, and cheeped and squeaked in her ear. The horrible Mouse-King came and sat on her shoulder, wheezed a blood-red foam out of all his seven mouths, and chattering and grinding his teeth, he hissed into Marie's ear:

"Hiss, hiss!—hand out your picture books—none of your scornful looks!—Give me your dresses—also your laces—or, if you don't, I'll bite Nutcracker—Fee, fi, fo, fum—his last hour is come!—Hee, hee—squeak, squeak!"

Marie was looking quite pale and upset when her mother said to her next morning:

"This horrid mouse hasn't been caught. But never mind, dear, we'll catch the nasty thing yet, never fear. If the traps don't work, Fritz shall fetch the gray cat from the baker's!"

As soon as Marie was alone, she went up to the glass cupboard, and said to Nutcracker, in a sobbing voice:

"Ah, my dear good Mr. Drosselmeier! Even if I give that horrid king of the mice all my picture books, and my new dress which the Christ Child gave me at Christmas as well, he's sure to go on asking for more. Soon I shan't have anything more left, and he'll want to eat me! What shall I do? What shall I do?"

As she was crying, she noticed that a great spot of blood had been left, since the eventful night of the battle, upon Nutcracker's neck. Since she had known that he was really young Mr. Drosselmeier, her godpapa's nephew, she had given up carrying him in her arms, and petting and kissing him. But now she took him carefully out of his shelf, and began to wipe off the spot of blood with her handkerchief. What were her feelings when she found that Nutcracker was growing warmer and warmer in her hand, and begin-

ning to move! She put him back into the cupboard as
fast as she could. His mouth began to wobble backwards and forwards, and he began to whisper, with
much difficulty:

"Ah, dearest Miss Stahlbaum—most precious of
friends! How much I owe you—*everything!* But don't,
don't sacrifice your picture books or pretty dresses
for me. Get me a sword. If you get me that, I'll
manage the rest."

Marie jumped for joy, now that she knew how to
help Nutcracker without further painful sacrifices. But
where was she to get hold of a sword for him? She
decided to talk to Fritz about it. That evening, when
their father and mother had gone out, and they two
were sitting beside the glass cupboard, she told him
what had passed between her and Nutcracker with
the king of the mice, and what it was Nutcracker
needed.

"As far as the sword is concerned," said Fritz, "I
can help Nutcracker. I placed an old colonel from my
cavalry men in retirement, so that he has no further
need for his sabre, which is sharp."

This colonel was fetched out and his sabre—a
bright silver sword—was taken off, and belted around
Nutcracker.

The next night Marie could not close her eyes she
was so worried. About midnight she thought she
heard a strange stirring and noise in the sitting-
room—a rustling and a clanging—and suddenly there
came a shrill "Queak!"

"The king of the mice! The king of the mice!" she cried, and jumped out of bed in terror. Everything was silent; but soon there came a gentle tapping at the door of her room, and a soft voice said:

"Please open the door, dearest Miss Stahlbaum! Don't be alarmed; it's good, happy news!"

It was Drosselmeier's voice—young Drosselmeier's. She threw on her dressing gown and opened the door. There stood Nutcracker, with his sword all covered with blood in his right hand, and a little candle in his left. When he saw Marie, he knelt down on one knee, and said:

"It was you, and you only, dearest lady, who inspired me with bravery, and gave me strength to do battle with the wicked mouse. The brutal king of the mice lies dying in his blood." With this Nutcracker took from his pocket the seven crowns of the Mouse-King and handed them as a gift to Marie.

Nutcracker now rose and said:

"Oh! my best beloved Miss Stahlbaum, if you would only take the trouble to follow me for a few steps, what beautiful things I could show you! Do come with me, dearest lady!"

CHAPTER 10

Toyland

"I WILL COME with you, dear Mr. Drosselmeier; but it mustn't be very far, and it won't do to be very long, because, you know, I haven't had any sleep yet," said Marie.

"Then we will go by the shortest way," said Nut-cracker.

He went on in front, followed by Marie, till he stopped before the big wardrobe. Marie was surprised to see that though it was generally shut, the doors of it were now wide open, so that she could see her father's travelling cloak hanging in the front. Nut-cracker climbed up this cloak, by the edgings and trimmings of it, so as to get hold of the big tassel which was fastened at the back of it by a thick cord. He gave this tassel a tug, and a pretty little ladder let itself down through one of the armholes of the cloak.

"Now, Miss Stahlbaum, step up that ladder," said Nutcracker. Marie did so. But as soon as she had got up through the armhole, and began to look out at the neck, a dazzling light came streaming over her, and she found herself standing on a lovely, sweet-scented meadow, from which millions of sparks were streaming upward, like the glitter of beautiful gems.

"This is Candy Meadow, where we are now," said Nutcracker. "But we'll go in at that gate there."

Marie looked up and saw a beautiful gateway on the meadow, only a few steps off. It seemed to be made of white, brown and raisin-colored marble; but when she came close to it she saw it was all of baked sugar-almonds and raisins. There was a gallery running round the upper part of it, made of sugar, and in this gallery six monkeys, dressed in red jackets, were playing delightful music on brass instruments. Marie, meanwhile, was walking along upon a beautiful pavement, a mosaic of candies of all colors. Soon the sweetest of odors came streaming from a beautiful little wood on both sides of the way. One could see all the gold and silver fruits hanging on the many-colored stems, and these stems and branches were all decorated with ribbons and bunches of flowers. And as the orange perfume wafted over, there was a sighing among the leaves and branches, and all the gold-leaf and tinsel rustled and tinkled like beautiful music.

"Oh, how charming this is!" cried Marie.

"This is Christmas Wood, dearest Miss Stahlbaum," said Nutcracker.

"Ah!" said Marie, "if I could only stay here for a little while! Oh, it is so lovely!"

Nutcracker clapped his hands, and immediately there appeared a number of little shepherds and shepherdesses, and hunters and huntresses, so white and delicate that you would have thought they were

made of pure sugar. They brought a beautiful gold reclining chair, laid a white satin cushion in it, and politely invited Marie to take a seat. As soon as she did so, the shepherds and shepherdesses danced a pretty ballet, to which the hunters and huntresses played music on their horns, and then they all disappeared among the trees.

"I must really apologize for the poor style in which this dance was performed, dearest Miss Stahlbaum," said Nutcracker. "These people all belong to our Wire Ballet Troupe, and can only do the same thing over and over again. Had we not better go on a little farther?"

"Oh, I enjoyed it immensely," said Marie, as she stood up and followed Nutcracker, who was leading the way. They went by the side of a gently rippling brook, which seemed to be what was giving out all the perfume which filled the wood.

"This is Orange Brook," said Nutcracker; "but, except for its sweet scent, it is nowhere nearly as fine a water as the River Lemonade, a beautiful broad stream, which falls—as this one does also—into the Almond-milk Sea."

And, indeed, Marie heard a louder plashing and rushing, and came in sight of the River Lemonade, which went rolling along in swelling waves of a yellowish color, between banks covered with shining green grass and bushes. A remarkable freshness and coolness came from this river. Not far from it a dark yellow stream crept slowly along, giving out a most delicious odor. A short distance farther, on the banks of this stream, stood a nice little village. The houses of this village, and the church, the parsonage, the barns and so forth, were all dark brown with golden roofs, and many of the walls looked as if they were plastered over with lemon peel and shelled almonds.

"This is Gingerton on the Honey River," said Nutcracker. They went on and came in sight of another little town, where the houses were all sorts of pretty colors. Nutcracker went on towards this town, and Marie heard a noise of merriment, and saw some thousands of nice little folks unloading a number of wagons which were drawn up in the market place.

"This is Bonbonville," Nutcracker said. "A group has just arrived from Paperland and the King of

Chocolate. These poor Bonbonville people have been attacked lately by the Fly-Admiral's forces, so they are covering their houses with their presents from Paperland, and making forts out of chocolate. But oh! dearest Miss Stahlbaum, let us be off to the big city."

He stepped quickly onwards, and Marie followed him. Soon a beautiful rosy vapor began to rise. She saw that this was reflected from rose-red, shining water, which went plashing and rushing away in front of them in wavelets of rosy silver. And on this delightful water, which kept widening and widening, like a lake, the loveliest swans were floating, white as silver, with collars of gold. And they were singing the most beautiful songs, to which little fish, glittering like diamonds, danced up and down in the rosy ripples.

"Oh!" cried Marie, "this must be the lake which Godpapa Drosselmeier was once going to make for me, and I am the girl who is to play with the swans."

Nutcracker gave a laugh, and said:

"My uncle could never make a thing of this kind. You would be much more likely to do it yourself. But don't let us bother about that. Rather let us go sailing over the water, Lake Rosa here, to the city."

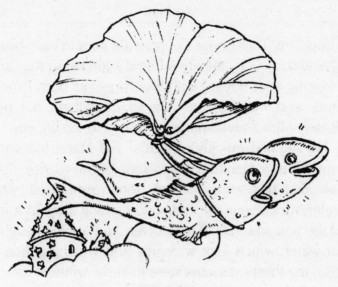

Chapter 11
The City

NUTCRACKER CLAPPED HIS little hands again, and the waves of Lake Rosa began to sound louder and to splash higher, and Marie became aware of a shell-shaped carriage approaching from the distance, made of glittering stones of every color, and drawn by two dolphins with scales of gold. Twelve dear little boys, with hats and jackets made of hummingbirds' feathers woven together, jumped to land, and carried first Marie and then Nutcracker, gently gliding above the water, into the carriage, which immediately began to skim over the lake. The two golden-scaled dolphins lifted their noses, and blew streams of crystals high in the air; and as these fell down in glittering, sparkling rainbows, there was a sound of two silvery voices singing, "Who comes over the rosy sea?—This is the fairy princess we long to see. Rosy waves dash—bright dolphins play—merrily, merrily on!"

Just then the twelve boys lifted Marie and Nutcracker out of the carriage and set them on shore. They found themselves in a small grove, almost more beautiful than Christmas Wood, everything glittered and sparkled so in it. And the fruit on the trees was wonderful and delicious, and not only of very strange colors, but with the most delicious scent.

"Ah," said Nutcracker, "here we are in Confection Grove, and over there lies the city."

Not only did the walls and towers of it shine in the brightest and most gorgeous colors, but the shapes and appearance of the buildings were like nothing to be seen on earth. Instead of roofs the houses had on beautiful crowns, and the towers were decorated with sculptures and carvings. As they passed in at the gateway, which looked as if it was made entirely of macaroons and sugared fruits, silver soldiers stood at attention, and a little man in fancy clothes threw himself upon Nutcracker's neck, crying:

"Welcome, dearest prince! Welcome to Sweetsburg!"

After a few paces more they were in a magnificent market place. All the houses which were round it were of sugar, with galleries towering above galleries; and in the center stood a lofty cake covered with frosting, with fountains round it spouting almond-milk, lemonade and other delicious drinks into the air. The gutters were running with cream, which you might have spooned up if you had liked. But prettier than all this were the delightful little people who were crowding about everywhere by the thousands, shouting, laughing, playing, and singing. There were beautifully dressed ladies and gentlemen, people of every kind to be found in the world.

Just then they watched as the Great Emperor passed along on his travelling throne, attended by ninety-three officers of the empire and seven hundred servants.

Then Marie and Nutcracker came before a castle shining in rosy light, with a hundred beautiful towers. Here and there upon its walls were bouquets of violets, tulips and carnations. The great dome of the central building, as well as the pyramid-like roofs of the towers, were set all over with thousands of sparkling gold and silver stars.

"Aha!" said Nutcracker, "here we are at Marzipan Castle at last."

At this moment, soft, beautiful music was heard, and out came twelve little attendants with lighted sticks, which they held in their little hands as torches. Each of their heads was a pearl, their bodies were emeralds and rubies and their feet were beautifully worked pure gold. After them came four ladies about the size of Marie's Miss Clara, but dressed brilliantly, as if they must be princesses. They embraced Nutcracker tenderly, and shed tears of gladness, saying, "Oh, dearest prince! beloved brother!"

Nutcracker wiped away his own tears of joy, and then he took Marie by the hand and said:

"This is Miss Marie Stahlbaum, the savior of my life. Had she not thrown her slipper just in the nick of time—had she not brought me a sword—I should have been lying in my cold grave at this moment, bitten to death by the king of the mice. I ask you to tell me, can Princess Pirlipat, princess though she is, compare for a moment with Miss Stahlbaum here in beauty, in goodness, in virtues of every kind? My answer is 'No.'"

All the ladies cried "No"; and they fell upon Marie's neck with sobs and tears, and cried: "Ah! noble savior of our beloved royal brother! Excellent Miss Stahlbaum!"

They now led Marie and Nutcracker into the castle, to a hall whose walls were made of sparkling crystal. But what delighted Marie most of all was the furniture. There were the most darling little chairs, tables, desks and so forth, standing about everywhere, all made of fine wood, covered with golden flowers. The princesses had Marie and Nutcracker sit down, and said that they would themselves prepare a banquet. So they went and brought little cups and dishes, and spoons, knives and forks, and other kitchen items of gold and silver. Then they fetched the most delightful fruits and sugar things—such as Marie had never seen the like of—and began to squeeze the fruit in the daintiest way with their little hands, and to grate the spices. What a magnificent banquet there was going to be! Marie wished she might be allowed to go and help the princesses. The prettiest of Nutcracker's sisters, just as if she had read the wishes of Marie's heart, handed her a little gold mortar, saying:

"Sweet friend, dear savior of our brother, would you mind pounding a little of this sugar-candy?"

Now as Marie went on pounding in the mortar with the utmost enjoyment—and the sound of it was like a lovely song—Nutcracker began to tell the story of all that had happened in that terrible fight between his forces and the army of the king of the mice; how he had the worst of it on account of the bad behavior of his troops; how the horrible mouse king had all but bitten him to death, so that Marie had to sacrifice a number of his subjects who were in his service and so on.

During all this storytelling, it seemed to Marie as if what Nutcracker was saying—and even the sound of her own mortar—kept growing more and more difficult to hear, seeming farther and farther away. Soon she saw a silver mist rising up all about, like clouds, in which the princesses, the attendants, Nutcracker and she herself were floating. And a strange singing and a buzzing and a humming began, which seemed to fade away in the distance; and then she seemed to be going up—up—up, as if on waves rising and swelling higher and higher, higher and higher, higher and higher.

Chapter 12

Conclusion

A<small>ND THEN</small> there came a "prr-poof," and Marie fell down from a great height.

That was a crash and a tumble!

However, she opened her eyes, and, lo and behold, there she was in her own bed! It was broad daylight, and her mother was standing at her bedside, saying:

"Well, what a sleep you have had! Breakfast has been ready for ever so long."

Of course, dear readers, you see how it was. Marie, amazed by all the wonderful things she had seen, had at last fallen asleep in Marzipan Castle, and the attendants, or perhaps the princesses themselves, had carried her home and put her to bed.

"Oh, mother darling," said Marie, "what a number of places young Mr. Drosselmeier has taken me to in the night, and what beautiful things I have seen!" And she told the story of it all, just as you have read about it.

Her mother listened, looking at her with wonder, and when she had finished, said:

"You have had a long, beautiful dream, Marie; but now you must put it all out of your head."

Marie insisted she had not been dreaming at all; so her mother took her to the glass cupboard, lifted out Nutcracker from his usual position on the third shelf, and said:

"You silly girl, how can you believe that this wooden figure can have life and motion?"

"Ah, mother," said Marie, "I know perfectly well that Nutcracker is young Mr. Drosselmeier from Nuremberg, Godpapa Drosselmeier's nephew."

Her father and mother both burst out laughing. Louise and even Fritz joined in the laughter. Marie ran into the next room, took the Mouse-King's seven crowns from her little box, and handed them to her mother, saying, "Look there, then, dear mother; those are the Mouse-King's seven crowns which young Mr. Drosselmeier gave me last night as a proof that he had got the victory."

Her mother gazed in amazement at the little crowns, which were made of some very brilliant, strange metal, and worked more beautifully than any human hands could have worked them. Dr. Stahlbaum could not stop looking at them with admiration and wonder, either, and both the father and the mother begged Marie to tell them where she really had got them from. But she could only repeat what she had said before; and when her father scolded her and accused her of lying, she began to cry and said, "Oh, dear me! What can I tell you except the truth!"

At this moment the door opened, and Godpapa Drosselmeier came in, saying, "Hello! hello! what's all this? My little Marie crying? What's all this?"

Dr. Stahlbaum told him all about it, and showed him the crowns. As soon as he had looked at them, however, he cried out:

"Nonsense! Nonsense! These are the crowns I used to wear on my watch-chain. I gave them as a present to Marie on her second birthday. Do you mean to tell me you don't remember?"

None of them *did* remember anything of the kind. But Marie ran up to her godpapa, and said, with tears in her eyes:

"You know all about this, Godpapa Drosselmeier; tell them. Let them know from your own lips that my Nutcracker is your nephew, young Mr. Drosselmeier from Nuremberg, and that it was he who gave me the crowns." But Drosselmeier made a very angry face, and muttered, "Stupid nonsense!" upon which Marie's father took her in front of him, and said:

"Now look here, Marie; let there be an end of all this foolish nonsense for once and for all; I'm not going to allow any more of it; and if ever I hear you say again that that idiotic, ugly Nutcracker is your godpapa's nephew, I shall throw, not only Nutcracker, but all your other playthings—even Miss Clara—out of the window."

Of course Marie dared not utter another word, but it was impossible for anyone who had seen all that she had seen to forget it. And I regret to say that even Fritz himself at once turned his back on his sister whenever she wanted to talk to him about the wonderful kingdom in which she had been so happy. Indeed, he kept saying, "Stupid goose!" at her.

Though not allowed to say anything more of her adventures, the memories of that fairy kingdom haunted Marie with sweet dreaminess, and the music of that delightful country still played tenderly in her ears.

It happened one day that Godpapa Drosselmeier was repairing one of the clocks in the house, and Marie was sitting beside the glass cupboard, sunk in her dreams and gazing at Nutcracker. All at once she said:

"Ah, dear Mr. Drosselmeier, if you really were alive, *I* shouldn't be like Princess Pirlipat and dislike you because you had had to give up being a nice handsome gentleman for my sake!"

"Stupid nonsense!" cried Godpapa Drosselmeier.

But, as he spoke, there came such a tremendous bang that Marie fell from her chair and fainted.

When she came back to her senses, her mother was tending her and saying, "How could you go and tumble off your chair like that, a big girl like you? Here is Godpapa Drosselmeier's nephew come from Nuremberg. See how good you can be."

Marie looked up. Her godpapa had on his yellow coat and his wig, and was smiling. By the hand he was holding a very small but very handsome young gentleman. His little face was red and white; he had on a beautiful red coat trimmed with gold lace, white silk stockings and shoes, with a lovely bouquet of flowers in his shirt frill. He had a pigtail hanging down his back. The little sword at his side seemed to be made of jewels, it sparkled so much, and the little hat under his arm was made of silk. He had fine manners, and had brought Marie a number of delightful toys—above all, the very same figures as those which the Mouse-King had eaten up—as well as a beautiful sabre for Fritz. He cracked nuts at the table for the whole party; the very hardest he could break. He placed them in his mouth with his left hand, tugged at his pigtail with his right, and crack! they fell in pieces.

Marie grew red as a rose at the sight of this charming young gentleman; and she grew redder still when after dinner he asked her to go with him to the glass cupboard in the living-room.

"Play nicely together, children," said Godpapa Drosselmeier.

As soon as young Drosselmeier was alone with Marie, he went down on one knee, and said:

"Ah! my most dearly beloved Miss Stahlbaum! See here at your feet the lucky Drosselmeier, whose life you saved here on this very spot. You were kind enough to say that *you* would not have disliked me, as Princess Pirlipat did, if I had been turned ugly for your sake. Immediately I stopped being a Nutcracker, and became again my old self. Ah! Most beautiful lady! Bless me with your hand; share with me my crown and kingdom, and rule with me in Marzipan Castle, for there I am now king."

Marie raised him from his knee, and said gently, "Dear Mr. Drosselmeier, you are a kind, nice gentleman; and as you rule over a delightful country of charming, pretty people, I accept your hand."

So then they were formally engaged; and when a year and a day had come and gone, they say he came and fetched her away in a golden coach, drawn by silver horses. At the wedding there danced twenty-two thousand of the most beautiful dolls and other figures, all glittering in pearls and diamonds; and Marie is to this day the queen of a kingdom where all kinds of sparkling Christmas Woods, and colored Marzipan Castles—in short, the most wonderful and beautiful things of every kind—are to be seen—by those who have the eyes to see them.

So this is the end of the tale of Nutcracker and the King of the Mice.